miffy and the artists

miffy and the artists

dick bruna

Have you ever been to a gallery to look at art? Or have you seen artworks anywhere else? Did you know that Dick Bruna really enjoyed looking at art? Before he became famous as the creator of Miffy, Dick Bruna was inspired by the work of artists such as Matisse, Léger, and Picasso.

Look closely at Dick Bruna's illustrations and the artworks in this book. What do you see? At first glance they might look nothing like Dick Bruna's work, but if you take your time, you'll start to see more and more similarities. What colors and objects can you see? What are the people wearing and doing? Can you spot things that look the same?

Join Miffy on an art adventure! Discover ways to look at art and get inspired by what you see. That's what this book is all about.

Take a look!

When Henri Matisse was an old man, he found it hard to hold a paintbrush. He decided to cut shapes out of paper instead. It is like drawing with scissors.

What shapes would you cut out to make a drawing?

Fernand Léger painted simple, bold shapes with
black outlines like you see in a coloring book.
He filled the shapes with bright colors.

Can you name the colors in both pictures?

Johannes Vermeer was fascinated by the ordinary
things people did at home every day.

What are Miffy and the milkmaid doing?

**Barbara Hepworth carved a mother and baby out of a big, pink pebble.
She made it look smooth and soft, so you would want to touch it.**

Whose eyes can you see?

**Pablo Picasso enjoyed playing with curvy shapes and patterns.
Some of his paintings look like giant jigsaw puzzles.**

Can you find the fingers of the musician strumming the guitar?

**Balloons have a funny way of making people feel happy.
Jeff Koons made an enormous balloon dog out of steel.
It is very heavy, but it looks like it could float up into the air.**

What will Miffy do with her balloon?

Jean-Michel Basquiat loved listening to jazz music.
The musician with the crown is playing
the trumpet as loud as he can.

Which trumpet player is making the loudest noise?

Andy Warhol liked to take photographs of himself and his friends.
He changed the colors of the photos to make them more mysterious.

Would you rather have a photo of yourself, or of your friends?

Yayoi Kusama loves polka dots. She likes to cover paintings, sculptures, buildings, furniture, and even her clothes with dots so that everything feels connected.

Do you think she would like Aunt Alice's dress?

Henri Rousseau
1891

Henri Rousseau loved painting tigers, monkeys, and tropical plants, but he never visited a real jungle.

How can you tell it's stormy?

Marcel Duchamp found a bicycle wheel and stuck it to a white stool.
He liked to turn the wheel and watch it spin.

Whirr. Do you like watching wheels spinning around too?

Frida Kahlo loved to look after animals. She had two pet monkeys, a parrot, three dogs, two turkeys, an eagle, a black cat, and a baby deer.

Which animal do you like the most?

René Magritte wasn't a magician, but his paintings
let him act like one. He chose simple objects like hats,
umbrellas, apples, and eggs, and made them do
magical things, like floating in the sky.

**Do you think the men are falling down like raindrops
or floating up like balloons?**

Nick Cave makes costumes out of fabric, buttons, feathers, and wire. All of his costumes hide the person inside, so you don't know who is wearing it.

Can you see who is dressed up as a ghost?

Bart van der Leck wanted to try out something new with his art by only using simple shapes and colors to create a picture of a family.

How many people are in Miffy's family? What about yours?

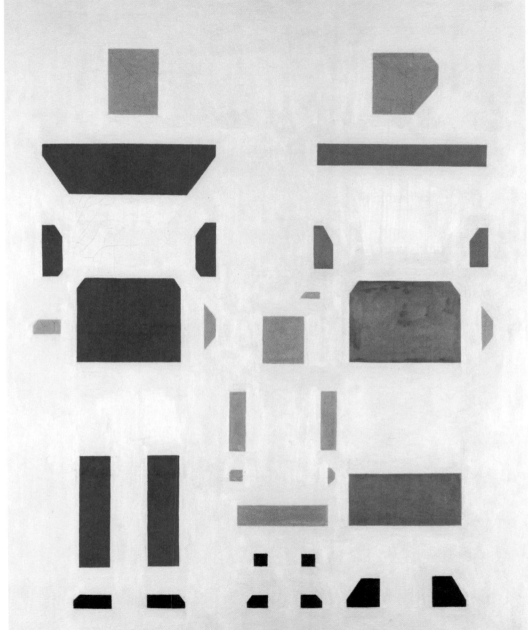

**Katsushika Hokusai wanted to know what it felt like
to row a boat in the middle of a big storm with giant waves.**

Are the sailors happy riding the giant waves?

Shibata Zeshin's favorite animals to paint and draw were little white mice. He wasn't scared of them.

Would you be scared of either of these mice?

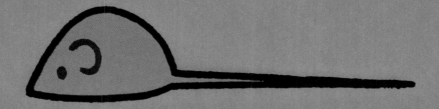

Keith Haring loved to move his body. It made him feel free.
He created bouncy-looking pictures of people dancing.

How do you like to move?

Alice Neel asked twin brothers if she could paint a picture of them.
The boys sat still for a very long time while she worked.

Do you think the children are happy waiting for her to finish?
What do you think Miffy is waiting for?

Berthe Morisot enjoyed painting outside near her village. One day, she asked her sister if she could paint her reading a book in a meadow of flowers.

Do you have a quiet place where you like to read?

Maria Sibylla Merian studied insects and plants, and painted detailed pictures to show the world what she had found. She was the first scientist to record a caterpillar changing into a butterfly.

Can you spot the little hairy caterpillar in the painting?

Vincent van Gogh cleaned his room and painted a picture of it to show his brother Theo.

Do you need to clean your room?

Kenojuak Ashevak drew pictures of birds that lived near
her home in the Arctic. The owl was her favorite.
She liked to think of herself as a happy owl.

What sort of bird would you like to be?

Joan Miró lived in the countryside where it is always very dark at night. He found it relaxing to gaze up at the stars and planets all around him.

Can you spot the crescent moon in the painting?

meet dick bruna

The first Miffy books were created with a pencil and
a brush. Dick Bruna drew a sketch, colored it in with
paint, and finally added the black contour lines.

Miffy's character design changed in 1963 and
with that Bruna's technique also changed, partly
at the request of his printer. It was necessary to
separate the black contour lines from the colors
filling them before they could be printed, which is
a time-consuming process. At first, Dick Bruna solved
this problem by painting a thin white line between
the black contours and the colors. But he only did
so briefly, before adopting a new working method
that involved drawing with scissors.

dick bruna at work

1. sketches
Dick Bruna first made a sketch on transparent paper.

2. final drawing
If he liked the drawing, he placed the sketch on top of a piece of watercolor paper, and then traced the image with a hard pencil. The pencil left an indent on the watercolor paper beneath.

3. black contours
Bruna then used a brush dipped in diluted poster paint to create the black contours. Rather than paint one continuous line, he meticulously applied the paint using short strokes to fill the indent. This brushwork, in combination with the watercolor paper, created the characteristic "heartbeat" in Bruna's lines. If he made a mistake, he started again from scratch. Corrections weren't part of his working method.

4. film
Once the contours were down on paper, the drawings were transferred onto a transparent film. Then Bruna would start thinking about color. Will Miffy's dress be blue or red? Should the balloon be yellow or green?

5. colors
Bruna developed his own color palette and the printer supplied him with sheets of paper saturated with his personal colors. These colors, which are only used in Bruna's books, may look like primary colors, but in fact they all contain a touch of black—a dab of darkness that distinguishes them from the standard red, blue, and yellow. He cut the personalized colored paper into shapes that matched each element of the illustration.

6. final illustration
If the blue dress wasn't right, he would cut out a red one. Bruna's method of drawing with scissors allowed him to change the colors easily, without having to redo the entire illustration. Finally, the film with the black contours was taped on top of the collage of colored shapes, and sent off to the printer.

meet the artists

Dimensions of works are given in centimeters and inches, height before width.

Henri Matisse
1869-1954, France

Henri Matisse was a painter and sculptor who was famous for his use of color. He spent a lot of time in Nice, in the South of France, and much of his art was inspired by his surroundings.

The Sheaf, 1953
Gouache on paper, cut and pasted on paper, mounted on canvas, 294 x 350 (115 ¾ x 137 ¾) Hammer Museum. Collection University of California, Los Angeles. Gift of Mr. and Mrs. Sidney F. Brody

Fernand Léger
1881-1955, France

Fernand Léger grew up on a cattle farm. He liked to create art that reminded him of fast-moving modern life, and developed his own unique style of painting that used bold, simplified shapes.

Two yellow butterflies on a scale, 1951
Oil on canvas, 92 x 73 (36 ¼ x 28 ¾) Centre Pompidou, Paris. Don de Lutèce Foundation, 1978. Photo Frank Buffetrille. All rights reserved 2025/Bridgeman Images. Fernand Léger © ADAGP, Paris and DACS, London 2025

Johannes Vermeer
1632-1675, Netherlands

Johannes Vermeer was a painter who lived in a city called Delft with his large family. He painted relaxing scenes of everyday life around him, as well as scenes from history, the Bible, and mythology.

The Milkmaid, c. 1660
Oil on canvas, 45.5 x 41 (17⅞ × 16⅛) Rijksmuseum, Amsterdam. Purchased with the support of the Vereniging Rembrandt

Barbara Hepworth
1903-1975, UK

Barbara Hepworth was a sculptor who created big, bold sculptures from wood and stone. She lived near the sea in a fishing village called St. Ives and took inspiration from the shapes she saw in the landscape.

Mother and Child, 1934
Pink ancaster stone
Photo Jerry Hardman-Jones. Courtesy The Hepworth Wakefield. Wakefield Permanent Art Collection/Barbara Hepworth © Bowness

Pablo Picasso
1881-1973, Spain
Pablo Picasso created
paintings, sculptures,
ceramics, and even
costumes and theater
sets. He helped to invent
Cubism—a way of making
art that shows 3D objects
from different angles in a
single image.

Harlequin Musician, 1924
Oil on canvas, 130 x 97.2
(51¼ x 38¼)
National Gallery of Art,
Washington, DC.
© Succession Picasso/DACS,
London 2025

Jeff Koons
b. 1955, U.S.
Jeff Koons is a sculptor
based in New York, famous
for creating giant versions
of everyday objects. He has
worked with celebrities, and
has created digital art that
can only be seen using a
mobile phone.

Balloon Dog (Blue), 1994-2000
Mirror-polished stainless steel
with transparent color coating,
307.34 x 363.22 x 114.3
(121 x 143 x 45)
The Broad Art Foundation,
Installation at The Museum
of Fine Arts, Boston.
Hayk Shalunts/Alamy
Stock Photo. © Jeff Koons.

Jean-Michel Basquiat
1960-1988, U.S.
Jean-Michel Basquiat was
a graffiti artist and painter
who stunned the art world
with his energetic paintings.
His work reflected the
experiences and history of
Black people in the U.S.

Trumpet, 1984
Acrylic and oil stick painting on
canvas, 152.4 x 152.4 (60 x 60)
Private Collection.
Photo ADAGP Images, Paris/
SCALA, Florence. © Estate of
Jean-Michel Basquiat. Licensed
by Artestar, New York

Andy Warhol
1928-1987, U.S.
Andy Warhol used
silkscreen prints to repeat
images of objects and
people on canvas.
He used bright color
combinations to make
his artworks as attention-
grabbing as billboards
and advertisements.

Self-Portrait, 1966
Silkscreen ink on synthetic
polymer paint on nine canvases,
171.7 x 171.7 (67⅝ x 67⅝)
The Museum of Modern Art,
New York. Gift of Philip Johnson.
Photo Fine Art Images/Bridgeman
Images. © 2025 The Andy Warhol
Foundation for the Visual Arts, Inc./
Licensed by DACS, London

**Yayoi Kusama
b. 1929, Japan**
Yayoi Kusama started painting and drawing with polka dots when she was ten years old. She creates dotted paintings, sculptures, fashion, and even entire rooms full of dots created by LED lights.

PUMPKIN, 2018
Painted Bronze, 145 x 150 x 150 (59⅛ x 57⅛ x 57⅛)
Courtesy the artist,
Ota Fine Arts and Victoria Miro.
© YAYOI KUSAMA

**Henri Rousseau
1844-1910, France**
Unlike other famous artists of his generation, Henri Rousseau did not train at an art school. He loved art and taught himself how to paint, choosing faraway locations and wild animals as his subject matter, even though he never traveled outside France during his lifetime.

Tiger in a Tropical Storm, 1891
Oil on canvas, 129.8 × 161.9 (51⅛ × 63¾)
The National Gallery, London.
Bought with the aid of a substantial donation from the Hon. Walter H. Annenberg, 1972.
Photo The National Gallery, London/Scala, Florence

**Marcel Duchamp
1887-1968, France**
Marcel Duchamp was perhaps the first artist to create a "readymade" artwork—a work of art made from objects that already existed. He proved that if you call something "art" then it becomes an artwork.

Bicycle Wheel, 1964 (replica of 1913 original).
Wheel, painted wood. 128.3 × 63.5 × 31.8 (50½ × 25 × 12½)
The Philadelphia Museum of Art.
Gift of Galleria Schwarz, 1964.
© Association Marcel Duchamp/ ADAGP, Paris and DACS, London 2025

**Frida Kahlo
1907-1954, Mexico**
Frida Kahlo liked to paint portraits of herself. Her Mexican culture was important to her and she reflected it in her clothes and artwork, painting herself wearing traditional Mexican clothing and jewelry.

Self Portrait with Thorn Necklace and Hummingbird, 1940
Oil on canvas on masonite, 61.3 x 47 (24¼ x 18⅝)
Harry Ransom Center, Austin, Texas.
Photo Bridgeman Images.

René Magritte
1898-1967, Belgium
René Magritte created art that looked strange and unrealistic, like something you would see in a dream. This is called Surrealist art. He wanted people to ask "what does that mean?" when they saw his paintings, even though there was not really an answer.

Golconda, 1953
Oil on canvas, 80 × 100.3 (31½ × 39½)
Photo Bridgeman Images.
René Magritte © ADAGP, Paris and DACS, London 2025

Nick Cave
b. 1959, U.S.
Nick Cave is very inspired by his African heritage, especially West African dance. He combines these with a love of fashion to create his artworks—costumes for dancing and performing in.

Sound Suit, 2010
Human hair and mannequin, 244 x 51 x 51 (96 x 29 x 20)
San Francisco Museum of Modern Art. Collection SFMOMA, Accessions Committee Fund purchase, 2010.
Photo James Prinz Photography.
© Nick Cave. Courtesy the artist and Jack Shainman Gallery, New York

Bart van der Leck
1876-1958, Netherlands
Bart van der Leck started his career making stained glass, then moved into interior design and advertising alongside creating his own artworks. Later in life, he applied his simplistic style to ceramics and tiles.

Family, 1921
Oil on canvas, 112 × 85 (44⅛ x 33½)
Collection Kröller-Müller Museum, Otterlo, the Netherlands.
Photo Rik Klein Gotink. Bart van der Leck © DACS 2025

Katsushika Hokusai
1760-1849, Japan
Katsushika Hokusai was a printmaker who lived and worked in Japan. He was famous for his landscapes and chose to make Japan's grandest mountain—Mount Fuji—appear tiny in comparison to the great wave, which is the subject of this print.

The Great Wave, c. 1830-32
Woodblock print, ink and color on paper, 25.7 x 37.9 (10⅛ x 15)
The Metropolitan Museum of Art, New York. H. O. Havemeyer Collection, Bequest of Mrs. H. O. Havemeyer, 1929

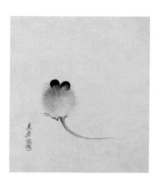

**Shibata Zeshin
1807-1891, Japan**
The painter Shibata Zeshin
was trained from the young
age of eleven to be a lacquer
artist. Lacquer painting is
a specialist technique that
involves applying layers
upon layers of liquid resin
to a surface to create an
image. Zeshin was a master
of his craft, and a famous
printmaker too.

Painting of a Mouse, c. 1800
Lacquer on paper, 19.4 x 16.8
(7¾ x 6⅝)
The British Museum, London.
Photo The Trustees of the
British Museum

**Keith Haring
1958-1990, U.S.**
Keith Haring was born in
Pennsylvania, U.S. but
lived and made most of his
artwork in New York. He
opened a "Pop Shop" in
1986 to sell items decorated
with his art, helping a wider
range of people to enjoy it.

Untitled (Pop Shop I series), 1987
Silkscreen print, edition of 200.
30.5 x 38.1 (12 x 15)
Keith Haring artwork © Keith
Haring Foundation

**Alice Neel
1900-1984, U.S.**
Alice Neel was a portrait
painter who loved to create
pictures of her friends,
family, other artists, and
poets, as well as strangers.
Her portraits show people
in a relaxed and informal
way, as they really are.

The Black Boys, 1967
Oil on canvas, 117.5 x 101.6
(46¼ x 40)
Tia Collection, Santa Fe,
New Mexico.
© The Estate of Alice Neel.
Courtesy The Estate of Alice Neel
and David Zwirner

**Berthe Morisot
1841-1895, France**
Berthe Morisot was the
first woman painter of the
Impressionist movement,
working alongside Édouard
Manet, and marrying
his brother Eugène. She
often painted her family
and friends in scenes of
everyday life.

Reading, 1873
Oil on fabric, 46 x 71.8
(18⅛ x 28¼)
Cleveland Museum of Art.
Gift of the Hanna Fund

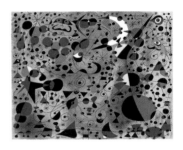

**Maria Sibylla Merian
1647-1717, Germany**
Maria Sibylla Merian was
interested in many areas
of natural science. She
journeyed for two years
with her daughter to
the east coast of South
America, to record the
many insects, plants, and
animals of the region.

*Chinese Vase with Roses,
Poppies and Carnations,* c. 1670-80
Copper-engraving, 26.7 x 18.7
(10⅝ x 7⅜)
Berlin State Museums,
Kupferstichkabinett

**Vincent van Gogh
1853-1890, Netherlands**
Born in the Netherlands,
Vincent van Gogh spent
much of his life in France.
He was inspired by nature
and his surroundings, but
also by Japanese woodcuts.
He created almost 2,000
paintings and drawings
over his career.

The Bedroom, 1888
Oil on canvas, 72.4 x 91.3
(28⅝ x 36)
Van Gogh Museum, Amsterdam
(Vincent van Gogh Foundation)

**Kenojuak Ashevak
1927-2013, Canada**
Kenojuak Ashevak was
one of the most famous
Inuit artists. She created
drawings, carvings, and
simple but striking prints
of people, Alaskan animals,
and symbols from Inuit
culture.

Preening Owl, 1995
Stonecut, 1995
49.5 x 73.7 (19½ x 29)
Reproduced by permission
of Dorset Fine Arts

**Joan Miró
1893-1983, Spain**
Joan Miro created highly
imaginative paintings,
sculptures and ceramics.
He said that he used color
to shape his art the way
musicians use musical
notes, or poets use words.
He is one of Spain's most
influential artists.

Constellations, 1959
From an illustrated book with one
lithograph and twenty-two
pochoir reproductions after
gouache, 35.5 x 43.6 (14 x 17¼)
The Museum of Modern Art,
New York. The Louis E.
Stern Collection.
© Successió Miró/ADAGP, Paris
and DACS London 2025

Publication licensed by Mercis Publishing bv, Amsterdam

Miffy and the Artists © 2025 Thames & Hudson Ltd, London

Text © 2025 Mercis Publishing bv
Illustrations by Dick Bruna © Mercis bv, 1953-2025
Photographs of Dick Bruna by Ferry André de la Porte © Mercis bv

First published in the United States of America in 2025
by Thames & Hudson Inc., 500 Fifth Avenue, New York,
New York 10110

Library of Congress Control Number 2024937778

ISBN 978-0-500-65378-4

Impression 01

Printed and bound in China by Leo Paper Products Ltd.

MIX
Paper | Supporting
responsible forestry
FSC® C020056
FSC
www.fsc.org

Be the first to know about our new releases,
exclusive content, and author events by visiting
thamesandhudson.com
thamesandhudsonusa.com
thamesandhudson.com.au